THIS WALKER BOOK BELONGS TO:

_____

_____

_____

For Jim Dowson,
a gentle man
N.D.

For Dave and Lucy
J.C.

First published 2004 by Walker Books Ltd
87 Vauxhall Walk, London SE11 5HJ

This edition published 2005

2 4 6 8 10 9 7 5 3 1

Text © 2004 Nick Dowson
Illustrations © 2004 Jane Chapman

The right of Nick Dowson and Jane Chapman to be
identified as author and illustrator respectively of this
work has been asserted by them in accordance with the
Copyright, Designs and Patents Act 1988

This book has been typeset in
Poliphilus and Caslon Antique

Printed in China

British Library Cataloguing in Publication Data:
a catalogue record for this book
is available from the British Library

ISBN 1-84428-742-4

www.walkerbooks.co.uk

WALKER BOOKS
AND SUBSIDIARIES
LONDON · BOSTON · SYDNEY · AUCKLAND

Tigress

Nick Dowson

illustrated by Jane Chapman

Twigs with whiskers?

A tree with a tail?

Or is it a tigress,

hiding?

Tigers are rarely seen, even though they can grow as big as Shetland ponies.
The tigers' bright stripes are perfect camouflage in their natural surroundings.

She can look exactly like a patch of forest, just by being there.
When she stalks slowly through leaves and shadows,
or crouches still in elephant grass,
her fiery stripy coat seems to vanish
like **magic.**

7

Bigger than your fist,
her pink nose sniffs the air.

Her ears turn to listen
for the smallest noise.

Bright as torches,
her large yellow eyes
gleam all around.

Tigers don't have a great sense of smell, but their eyesight is six times better than ours, and they have amazing hearing.

8

She's searching for a new den.

Somewhere safe for young cubs.

Smooth as a river she moves;
her plate-sized paws press the ground
but don't make a sound.
When she runs, strong muscles stretch
and ripple her body like wind on water.

She finds an untidy pile of rocks across the clearing,
full of dark cracks and crevices.
Perfect hiding for tiny cubs.

She will bring them here tonight.

Mother tigers look after their cubs alone;
so when the mothers hunt, the cubs are left unprotected.
Changing dens helps to fool predators like leopards
or wild dogs, who may kill the cubs.

Back at the old den the cubs are snuggled deep in shaded sleep.

Their bright white ear spots wink out like magic eyes.

With rough, wet licks from her long tongue, the tigress stirs them awake.

12

No one knows for sure why tigers have ear spots.
They may help small cubs to follow their mother.
Or perhaps they are flashed as
a warning to other tigers.

Grooming keeps their fur sleek and clean, but the wriggling cubs are eager to feed.
Small as a sugar bag at birth, baby tigers drink rich mother's milk
and fill up like fat, furry cushions.

These two are too small to walk far, so the tigress uses tooth-power.
The gentle mother carries her dangling cubs, one by one,
to safety at the new den.

Tiger cubs have loose skin
on their necks, which makes
them easy to lift.

15

While the tigress hunts for food,
brother and sister stalk,
stretch and snarl.
Teeth bared, heads together,

this could be a tiger fight.

But their knife-sharp claws are
sheathed this time, and don't draw
blood. The cubs are six months
old now — when they are
older their claws will cut
deep into the hardest wood,
or the tough hide of
their prey.

Tigers can get badly hurt in fights,
so they usually avoid each other. Tigers
find their own territory, which they mark
by scratching trees and rocks and by leaving
their scent on bushes and leaves.

Sharp grass stems scratch three empty bellies.
For days mother and cubs have chewed old
skin and crunched cold bones.
The tigress needs a big kill, and now
the hungry year-old cubs are too big
and strong to play-hunt by the den.

A wild pig's big, bristly head bends
as his snout shoves and snuffles for grubs.
Fierce eyes burning, noses wrinkling
with his smell, the three tigers creep
closer with soft, slow steps
and crouch, still as stone.

*Young tigers start eating
meat at around eight weeks old.
They start hunting when they are half-grown.*

19

The cubs' whiskers quiver. Their hearts thump loud as drums.
Like fire the roaring tigress leaps and falls
in a crush of teeth and muscle,
and, mouths open, her snarling
cubs rush in.

*Tigers are good hunters, but even they only catch their
prey on average three times out of every ten attempts.
Tiger cubs always eat first, and if there's not much
meat the mother may not feed at all.*

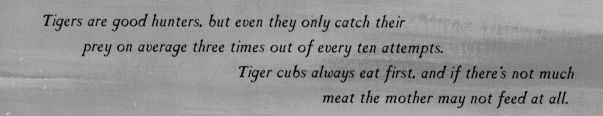

Now the family will eat its fill.

The sun turns tiger fur oven-hot,
so after the big feed and a sleep,
the tigress heads for the lake.

While her cubs splash and
swim, she floats in cool,
green water to soak
away the heat.

Tigers are among the few big cats
to enjoy swimming.

Between eighteen months and three years old, tigers leave their old territory and find a new territory of their own.

Three sleek tigers prowl the midnight forest.

The tigress taught the two cubs all her tricks.

Now, at eighteen months, they must find their own homes without her.

A pattern of gliding stripes slides into the trees
and the mother disappears.
Brother nuzzles sister for the last time, and walks away.

She watches the forest swallow his tail.

Then she turns, silently crosses the moonlit clearing.

And, just like her magic mother, the young tigress

vanishes.

About Tigers

For years tigers were hunted and killed in large numbers, and of the eight kinds that once prowled the forests, only five survive. There are fewer than 6,000 tigers alive today, scattered across parts of China, Indonesia, India and south-east Russia.

Today tigers are protected, but poachers still kill them; and people want the land where they live, threatening our last wild tigers with total extinction.

Index

Look up the pages to find out about all these tiger things. Don't forget to look at both kinds of word —

this kind and *this kind*.

About the Author
Nick Dowson is a teacher and this is his first book. He has always been interested in tigers. "Tigers are one of the creatures that sometimes roam my dreams," Nick says. "They are completely captivating and remain mysterious. I'd hate to see them pushed off the world."

About the Illustrator
Jane Chapman is the award-winning illustrator of many books, including *The Emperor's Egg* and *One Tiny Turtle*. She thinks that tiger mums have a really tough time in India's climate. "I would be so grumpy in all that heat," she says. "No wonder they spend so much time in the water!"

NOTES FOR TEACHERS

The **READ AND WONDER** series is an innovative and versatile resource for reading, thinking and discovery. Each book invites children to become excited about a topic, see how varied information books can be, and want to find out more.

☞ **Reading aloud** The story form makes these books ideal for reading aloud – in their own right or as part of a cross-curricular topic, to a child or to a whole class. After you've introduced children to the books in this way, they can revisit and enjoy them again and again.

☞ **Shared reading** Big Book editions are available for several titles, so children can read along, discuss the topic, and comment on the different ways information is presented – to wonder together.

☞ **Group and guided reading** Children need to experience a range of reading materials. Information books like these help develop the skills of reading to learn, as part of learning to read. With the support of a reading group, children can become confident, flexible readers.

☞ **Paired reading** It's fun to take turns to read the information in the main text or in the captions. With a partner, children can explore the pages to satisfy their curiosity and build their understanding.

☞ **Individual reading** These books can be read for interest and pleasure by children at home and in school.

☞ **Research** Once children have been introduced to these books through reading aloud, they can use them for independent or group research, as part of a curricular topic.

☞ **Children's own writing** You can offer these books as strong models for children's own information writing. They can record their observations and findings about a topic, make field notes and sketches, and add extra snippets of information for the reader.

Above all, Read and Wonders are to be enjoyed, and encourage children to develop a lasting curiosity about the world they live in.

Sue Ellis, Centre for Language in Primary Education